Jennie Hall

Buried Cities
Volume 3

Jennie Hall

Buried Cities
Volume 3

1st Edition | ISBN: 978-3-75235-900-8

Place of Publication: Frankfurt am Main, Germany

Year of Publication: 2020

Outlook Verlag GmbH, Germany.

Part 3, Mycenae

BURIED CITIES

BY

JENNIE HALL

HOW A LOST CITY WAS FOUND

Thirty years ago a little group of people stood on a hill in Greece. The hilltop was covered with soft soil. The summer sun had dried the grass and flowers, but little bushes grew thick over the ground. In this way the hill was like an ordinary hill, but all around the edge of it ran the broken ring of a great wall. In some places it stood thirty feet above the earth. Here and there it was twenty feet thick. It was built of huge stones. At one place a tower stood up. In another two stone lions stood on guard. It was these ruined walls that interested the people on the hill. One of the men was a Greek. A red fez was on his head. He wore an embroidered jacket and loose white sleeves. A stiff kilted skirt hung to his knees. He was pointing about at the wall and talking in Greek to a lady and gentleman. They were visitors, come to see these ruins of Mycenae.

"Once, long, long ago," he was saying, "a great city was inside these walls. Giants built the walls. See the huge stones. Only giants could lift them. It was a city of giants. See their great ovens."

He pointed down the hill at a doorway in the earth. "You cannot see well from here. I will take you down. We can look in. A great dome, built of stone, is buried in the earth. A passage leads into it, but it is filled with dirt. We can look down through the broken top. The room inside is bigger than my whole house. There giants used to bake their bread. Once a wicked Turk came here. He was afraid of nothing. He said, 'The giants' treasure lies in this oven. I will have it.' So he sent men down. But they found only broken pieces of carved marble—no gold."

While the guide talked, the gentleman was tramping about the walls. He peered into all the dark corners. He thrust a stick into every hole. He rubbed the stones with his hands. At last he turned to his guide.

"You are right," he said. "There was once a great city inside these walls. Houses were crowded together on this hill where we stand. Men and women walked the streets of a city that is buried under our feet, but they were not giants. They were beautiful women and handsome men.

"It was a famous old city, this Mycenae. Poets sang songs about her. I have read those old songs. They tell of Agamemnon, its king, and his war against Troy. They call him the king of men. They tell of his gold-decked palace and his rich treasures and the thick walls of his city.

"But Agamemnon died, and weak kings sat in his palace. The warriors of Mycenae grew few, and after hundreds of years, when the city was old and weak, her enemies conquered her. They broke her walls, they threw down her houses, they drove out her people. Mycenae became a mass of empty ruins. For two thousand years the dry winds of summer blew dust over her palace

2

floors. The rains of winter and spring washed down mud from her acropolis into her streets and houses. Winged seeds flew into the cracks of her walls and into the corners of her ruined buildings. There they sprouted and grew, and at last flowers and grass covered the ruins. Now only these broken walls remain. You feed your sheep in the city of Agamemnon. Down there on the hillside farmers have planted grain above ancient palaces. But I will uncover this wonderful city. You shall see! You shall see how your ancestors lived.

"Oh! for years I have longed to see this place. When I was a little boy in Germany my father told me the old stories of Troy, and he told me of how great cities were buried. My heart burned to see them. Then, one night, I heard a man recite some of the lines of Homer. I loved the beautiful Greek words. I made him say them over and over. I wept because I was not a Greek. I said to myself, 'I will see Greece! I will study Greek. I will work hard. I will make a bankful of money. Then I will go to Greece. I will uncover Troy-city and see Priam's palace. I will uncover Mycenae and see Agamemnon's grave.' I have come. I have uncovered Troy. Now I am here. I will come again and bring workmen with me. You shall see wonders." He walked excitedly around and around the ruins. He told stories of the old city. He asked his wife to recite the old tales of Homer. She half sang the beautiful Greek words. Her husband's eyes grew wet as he listened.

This man's name was Dr. Henry Schliemann. He kept his word. He went away but he came again in a few years. He hired men and horse-carts. He rented houses in the little village. Myceae was a busy place again after three thousand years. More than a hundred men were digging on the top of this hill. They wore the fezes and kilts of the modern Greek. Little two-wheeled horse-carts creaked about, loading and dumping.

Some of the men were working about the wall near the stone lions.

"This is the great gate of the city," said Dr. Schliemann. "Here the king and his warriors used to march through, thousands of years ago. But it is filled up with dirt. We must clear it out. We must get down to the very stones they trod."

But it was slow work. The men found the earth full of great stone blocks. They had to dig around them carefully, so that Dr. Schliemann might see what they were.

"How did so many great stones come here?" they said among themselves.

Then Dr. Schliemann told them. He pointed to the wall above the gate.

"Once, long, long ago," he said, "the warriors of Mycenae stood up there. Down here stood an army—the men of Argos, their enemies. The men of

Argos battered at the gate. They shot arrows at the men of Mycenae, and the men of Mycenae shot at the Argives, and they threw down great stones upon them. See, here is one of those broken stones, and here, and here. After a long time the people of Mycenae had no food left in their city. Their warriors fainted from hunger. Then the Argives beat down the gate. They rushed into the city and drove out the people. They did not want men ever again to live in Mycenae, so they took crowbars and tried to tear down the wall. A few stones they knocked off. See, here, and here, and here they are, where they fell off the wall. But these great stones are very heavy. This one must weigh a hundred twenty tons,—more than all the people of your village. So the Argives gave up the attempt, and there stand the walls yet. Then the rain washed down the dirt from the hill and covered these great stones, and now we are digging them out again."

The men worked at the gateway for many weeks. At last all the dirt and the blocks had been cleared away. The tall gateway stood open. A hole was in the stone door-casing at top and bottom. Schliemann put his hand into it.

"See!" he cried. "Here turned the wooden hinge of the gate."

He pointed to another large hole on the side of the casing. "Here the gatekeeper thrust in the beam to hold the gate shut."

Just inside the gate he found the little room where the keeper had stayed. He found also two little sentry boxes high up on the wall. Here guards had stood and looked over the country, keeping watch against enemies. From the gate the wall bent around the edge of the hilltop, shutting it in. In two places had been towers for watchmen. Inside this great wall the king's palace and a few houses had been safe. Outside, other houses had been built. But in time of war all the people had flocked into the fortress. The gate had been shut. The warriors had stood on the wall to defend their city.

But while some of Dr. Schliemann's men were digging at the gateway and the wall, others were working outside the city. They were making a great hole, a hundred and thirteen feet square. They put the dirt into baskets and carried it to the little carts to be hauled away. And always Dr. Schliemann and his wife worked with them. From morning until dusk every day they were there. It was August, and the sun was hot. The wind blew dust into their faces and made their eyes sore, and yet they were happy. Every day they found some little thing that excited them,—a terra cotta goblet, a broken piece of a bone lyre, a bronze ax, the ashes of an ancient fire.

At first Dr. Schliemann and his wife had fingered over every spadeful of dirt. There might be something precious in it. "Dig carefully, carefully!" Dr. Schliemann had said to the workmen. "Nothing must be broken. Nothing must be lost. I must see everything. Perhaps a bit of a broken vase may tell a wonderful story."

But during this work of many weeks he had taught his workmen how to dig. Now each man looked over every spadeful of earth himself, as he dug it up. He took out every scrap of stone or wood or pottery or metal and gave it to Schliemann or his wife. So the excavators had only to study these things and to tell the men where to work. When a man struck some new thing with his spade, he called out. Then the excavators ran to that place and dug with their own hands. When anything was found, Dr. Schliemann sent it to the village. There it was kept in a house under guard. At night Dr. Schliemann drew plans of Mycenae. He read again old Greek books about the city. As he read he studied his plans. He wrote and wrote.

"As soon as possible, I must tell the world about what we find," he said to his wife. "People will love my book, because they love the stories of Homer."

There had been four months of hard work. A few precious things had been uncovered,—a few of bronze and clay, a few of gold, some carved gravestones. But were these the wonders Schliemann had promised? Was this to be all? They had dug down more than twenty feet. A few more days, and they would probably reach the solid rock. There could be nothing below that. November was rainy and disagreeable. The men had to work in the mud and wet. There was much disappointment on the hilltop.

Then one day a spade grated on gravel. Once before that had happened, and they had found gold below. They called out to Dr. Schliemann. He and his wife came quickly. Fire leaped into Schliemann's eyes.

"Stop!" he said. "Now I will dig. Spades are too clumsy."

So he and his wife dropped upon their knees in the mud. They dug with their knives. Carefully, bit by bit, they lifted the dirt. All at once there was a glint of gold.

"Do not touch it!" cried Schliemann, "we must see it all at once. What will it be?"

So they dug on. The men stood about watching. Every now and then they shouted out, when some wonderful thing was uncovered, and Schliemann would stop work and cry,

"Did not I tell you? Is it not worth the work?"

At last they had lifted off all the earth and gravel. There was a great mass of golden things—golden hairpins, and bracelets, and great golden earrings like wreaths of yellow flowers, and necklaces with pictures of warriors embossed in the gold, and brooches in the shape of stags' heads. There were gold covers for buttons, and every one was molded into some beautiful design of crest or circle or flower or cuttle-fish.

And among them lay the bones of three persons. Across the forehead of one was a diadem of gold, worked into designs of flowers. "See!" cried Schliemann, "these are queens. See their crowns, their scepters."

For near the hands lay golden scepters, with crystal balls.

And there were golden boxes with covers. Perhaps long ago, one of these queens had kept her jewels in them. There was a golden drinking cup with swimming fish on its sides. There were vases of bronze and silver and gold. There was a pile of gold and amber beads, lying where they had fallen when the string had rotted away from the queenly neck. And scattered all over the bodies and under them were thin flakes of gold in the shapes of flowers, butterflies, grasshoppers, swans, eagles, leaves. It seemed as though a golden tree had shed its leaves into the grave.

"Think! Think! Think!" cried Schliemann. "These delicate lovely things have lain buried here for three thousand years. You have pastured your sheep above them. Once queens wore them and walked the streets we are uncovering."

The news of the find spread like wildfire over the country. Thousands of people came to visit the buried city. It was the most wonderful treasure that had ever been found. The king of Athens sent soldiers to guard the place. They camped on the acropolis. Their fires blazed there at night. Schliemann telegraphed to the king:

"With great joy I announce to your majesty that I have discovered the tombs which old stories say are the graves of Agamemnon and his followers. I have found in them great treasures in the shape of ancient things in pure gold. These treasures, alone, are enough to fill a great museum. It will be the most wonderful collection in the world. During the centuries to come it will draw visitors from all over the earth to Greece. I am working for the joy of the work, not for money. So I give this treasure, with much happiness, to Greece. May it be the corner stone of great good fortune for her."

The work went on, and soon they found another grave, even more wonderful. Here lay five people—two of them women, three of them warriors. Golden masks covered the faces of the men. Two wore golden breastplates. The gold clasp of the greave was still around one knee. Near one man lay a golden crown and a sceptre, and a sword belt of gold. There was a heap of stone arrowheads, and a pile of twenty bronze swords and daggers. One had a picture of a lion hunt inlaid in gold. The wooden handles of the swords and daggers were rotted away, but the gold nails that had fastened them lay there, and the gold dust that had gilded them. Near the warriors' hands were drinking cups of heavy gold. There were seal rings with carved stones. There was the silver mask of an ox head with golden horns, and the golden mask of a lion's head. And scattered over everything were buttons, and ribbons, and leaves, and flowers of gold.

Schliemann gazed at the swords with burning eyes.

"The heroes of Troy have used these swords," he said to his wife, "Perhaps Achilles himself has handled them." He looked long at the golden masks of kingly faces.

"I believe that one of these masks covered the face of Agamemnon. I believe I am kneeling at the side of the king of men," he said in a hushed voice.

Why were all these things there? Thousands of years before, when their king had died, the people had grieved.

"He is going to the land of the dead," they had thought. "It is a dull place. We will send gifts with him to cheer his heart. He must have lions to hunt and swords to kill them. He must have cattle to eat. He must have his golden cup for wine."

So they had put these things into the grave, thinking that the king could take them with him. They even had put in food, for Schliemann found oyster shells buried there. And they had thought that a king, even in the land of the dead, must have servants to work for him. So they had sacrificed slaves, and had sent them with their lord. Schliemann found their bones above the grave. And besides the silver mask of the ox head they had sent real cattle. After the king had been laid in his grave, they had killed oxen before the altar. Part they had burned in the sacred fire for the dead king, and part the people had eaten for the funeral feast. These bones and ashes, too, Schliemann found. For a long, long time the people had not forgotten their dead chiefs. Every year they had sacrificed oxen to them. They had set up gravestones for them, and after a while they had heaped great mounds over their graves.

That was a wonderful old world at Mycenae. The king's palace sat on a hill. It was not one building, but many—a great hall where the warriors ate, the women's large room where they worked, two houses of many bedrooms, treasure vaults, a bath, storehouses. Narrow passages led from room to room. Flat roofs of thatch and clay covered all. And there were open courts with porches about the sides. The floors of the court were of tinted concrete. Sometimes they were inlaid with colored stones. The walls of the great hall had a painted frieze running about them. And around the whole palace went a thick stone wall.

One such old palace has been uncovered at Tiryns near Mycenae. To-day a visitor can walk there through the house of an ancient king. The watchman is not there, so the stranger goes through the strong old gateway. He stands in the courtyard, where the young men used to play games. He steps on the very floor they trod. He sees the stone bases of columns about him. The wooden pillars have rotted away, but he imagines them holding a porch roof, and he sees the men resting in the shade. He walks into the great room where the warriors feasted. He sees the hearth in the middle and imagines the fire blazing there. He looks into the bathroom with its sloping stone floor and its holes to drain off the water. He imagines Greek maidens coming to the door with vases of water on their heads. He walks through the long, winding passages and into room after room. "The children of those old days must have had trouble finding their way about in this big palace," he thinks.

Such was the palace of the king. Below it lay many poorer houses, inside the walls and out. We can imagine men and women walking about this city. We raise the warriors from their graves. They carry their golden cups in their hands. Their rings glisten on their fingers, and their bracelets on their arms. Perhaps, instead of the golden armor, they wear breastplates of bronze of the same shape, but these same swords hang at their sides. We look at their golden masks and see their straight noses and their short beards. We study the carving on their gravestones, and we see their two-wheeled chariots and their prancing horses. We look at the carved gems of their seal rings and see them fighting or killing lions. We look at their embossed drinking cups, and we see them catching the wild bulls in nets. We gaze at the great walls of Mycenae, and wonder what machines they had for lifting such heavy stones. We look at a certain silver vase, and see warriors fighting before this very wall. We see all the beautiful work in gold and silver and gems and ivory, and we think, "Those men of old Mycenae were artists."

PICTURES OF MYCENAE

THE CIRCLE OF ROYAL TOMBS.

Digging within this circle, Dr. Schliemann found the famous treasure of golden gifts to the dead, which he gave to Greece. In the Museum at Athens you can see these wonderful things. (From a photograph in the Metropolitan Museum.)

DR. AND MRS. SCHLIEMANN AT WORK.

This picture is taken from Dr. Schliemann's own book on his work.

THE GATE OF LIONS.

The stone over the gateway is immensely strong. But the wall builders were afraid to pile too great a weight upon it. So they left a triangular space above it. You can see how they cut the big stones with slanting ends to do this. This triangle they filled with a thinner stone carved with two lions. The lions' heads are gone. They were made separately, perhaps of bronze, and stood away from the stone looking out at people approaching the gate.

INSIDE THE TREASURY OF ATREUS.

No wonder the untaught modern Greeks thought that this was a giants' oven, where the giants baked their bread. But learned men have shown that it was connected with a tomb, and that in this room the men of Mycenae worshipped their dead. It was very wonderfully made and beautifully ornamented. The big stone over the doorway was nearly thirty feet long, and weighs a hundred and twenty tons. Men came to this beehive tomb in the old days of Mycenae, down a long passage with a high stone wall on either side. The doorway was decorated with many-colored marbles and beautiful bronze plates. The inside was ornamented, too, and there was an altar in there.

THE INTERIOR OF THE PALACE.

From these ruins and relics, we know much about the art of the Mycenaeans, something about their government, their trade, their religion, their home life, their amusements, and their ways of fighting, though they lived three thousand years ago. If a great modern city should be buried, and men should dig it up three thousand years later, what do you think they will say about us?

GOLD MASK.

This mask was still on the face of the dead king. The artist tried to make the mask look just as the great king himself had looked, but this was very hard to do.

A COW'S HEAD OF SILVER.

The king's people put into his grave this silver mask of an ox head with golden horns. It was a symbol of the cattle sacrificed for the dead. There is a gold rosette between the eyes. The mouth, muzzle, eyes and ears are gilded. In Homer's Iliad, which is the story of the Trojan war, Diomede says, "To thee will I sacrifice a yearling heifer, broad at brow, unbroken, that never yet hath man led beneath the yoke. Her will I sacrifice to thee, and gild her horns with gold."

THE WARRIOR VASE.

This vase was made of clay and baked. Then the artist painted figures on it with colored earth. This was so long ago that men had not learned to draw very well, but we like the vase because the potter made it such a beautiful shape, and because we learn from it how the warriors of early Mycenae dressed. Under their armor they wore short chitons with fringe at the bottom, and long sleeves, and they carried strangely shaped shields and short spears or long lances. Do you think those are knapsacks tied to the lances?

BRONZE HELMETS.

These may have been worn by King Agamemnon, or by the Trojan warriors. They are now in the Metropolitan Museum in New York.

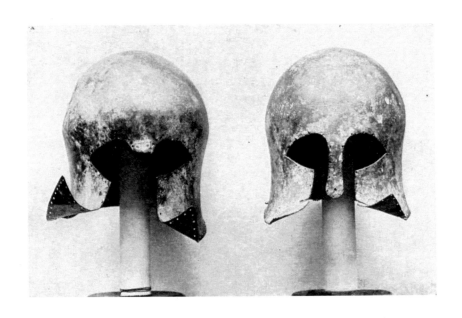

GEM FROM MYCENAE.

Early men made many pictures much like this—a pillar guarded by an animal on each side.

BRONZE DAGGERS.

It would take a very skilfull man to-day, a man who was both goldsmith and artist, to make such daggers as men found at Mycenae. First the blade was made. Then the artist took a separate sheet of bronze for his design. This sheet he enamelled, and on it he inlaid his design. On one of these daggers we see five hunters fighting three lions. Two of the lions are running away. One lion is pouncing upon a hunter, but his friends are coming to help him. If you could turn this dagger over, you would see a lion chasing five gazelles. The artist used pure gold for the bodies of the hunters and the lions; he used electron, an alloy of gold and silver, for the hunters' shields and their trousers; and he made the men's hair, the lions' manes, and the rims of the shields, of some black substance. When the picture was finished on the plate, he set the plate into the blade, and riveted on the handle. On the smaller dagger we see three lions running.

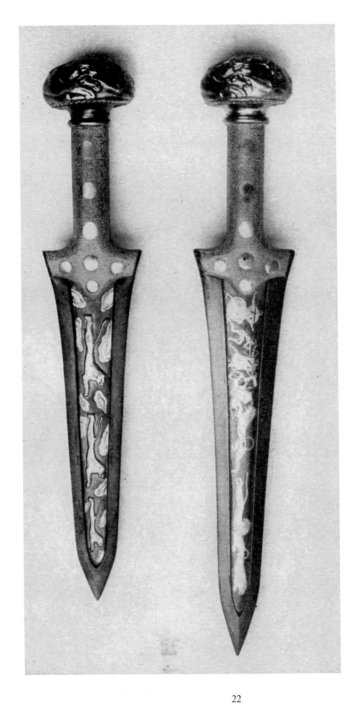

CARVED IVORY HEAD.

It shows the kind of helmet used in Mycenae. Do you think the button at the top may have had a socket for a horse hair plume?

BRONZE BROOCHES.

These brooches were like modern safety pins, and were used to fasten the chlamys at the shoulder. The chlamys was a heavy woolen shawl, red or purple.

ONE OF THE CUPS FOUND AT VAPHIO.

Some people say that these cups are the most wonderful things that have been found, made by Mycenaean artists. Some people say that no goldsmiths in the world since then, unless perhaps in Italy in the fifteenth century, have done such lovely work. The goldsmith took a plate of gold and hammered his design into it from the wrong side. Then he riveted the two ends together where the handle was to go, and lined the cup with a smooth gold plate. One cup shows some hunters trying to catch wild bulls with a net. One great bull is caught in the net. One is leaping clear over it. And a third bull is tossing a hunter on his horns. On the other cup the artist shows some bulls quietly grazing in the forest, while another one is being led away to sacrifice.

The Vaphian cups are now in the National museum in Athens. They were found in a "bee-hive" tomb at Vaphio, an ancient site in Greece, not far from Sparta. It is thought that they were not made there, but in Crete.

PLATES.

At Mycenae were found seven hundred and one large round plates of gold, decorated with cuttlefish, flowers, butterflies, and other designs.

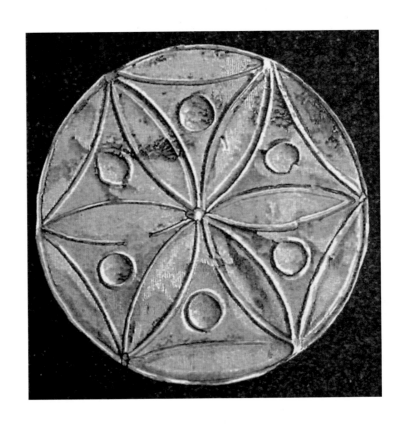

GOLD ORNAMENT.

MYCENAE IN THE DISTANCE.